PJ MASKS

PJ MASKS SAVE THE SLEEPOVER!

Based on the episode
"PJ Party Crasher"

Ready-to-Read

Simon Spotlight
New York London Toronto Sydney New Delhi

Licensed by:

SIMON SPOTLIGHT
An imprint of Simon & Schuster Children's Publishing Division
1230 Avenue of the Americas, New York, New York 10020
This Simon Spotlight edition July 2021
Adapted by May Nakamura from the series PJ Masks

Manufactured in the United States of America 0621 LAK
10 9 8 7 6 5 4 3 2 1
ISBN 978-1-5344-8569-3 (hc)
ISBN 978-1-5344-8568-6 (pbk)
ISBN 978-1-5344-8570-9 (ebook)

Amaya is having
a sleepover tonight.
There will be dress-up,
games, movies, snacks,
and fun!

Moths swoop in
and steal an invitation!
Are they moths from Luna Girl?
Will she show up
and ruin the party?

This is a job
for the PJ Masks!

Amaya becomes Owlette!

Connor becomes

Catboy!

Greg becomes

Gekko!

They are the PJ Masks!

Jenny and Marie
arrive at the sleepover.

Catboy and Gekko
keep watch for Luna Girl.

Then Luna Girl arrives.

“This sleepover is for guests only,” Owlette says.

Luna Girl gives her
the stolen invitation.
But Owlette says no.

The sleepover continues without Luna Girl.

Luna Girl has a new plan.

She steals the party food.

She even captures

Gekko and Catboy in bubbles!

Next, she captures

Jenny and Marie!

"Owl Wing Wind!"

says Owlette.

Jenny and Marie
are safe from Luna Girl.

But then Motsuki decides she wants her own party . . . on the moon!

She steals
all the food.
Catboy and Gekko
are in trouble too!

“I started this mess.
I should help fix it,”
Luna Girl says.

It is time to be heroes!

Luna Girl pops the bubbles.

Owlette catches Catboy.

Luna Girl catches Gekko.

Everyone is safe!

But Luna Girl is sad.
She is still not invited
to the sleepover.

Owlette did not mean to

hurt her feelings.

It is not too late

to have fun together!

The sleepover begins again.
Luna Girl, Catboy,
and Gekko join in too.

“Smile!” Owlette says.

She takes a photo.

PJ Masks all shout hooray!
Because in the night
they saved the day . . .
and the sleepover!